The INVITATION

Nicola Smee

Collins

For
Richard and Fara
Maddy Farrell
Michael
Olly, Milo
and Leo . . .
with love

William Collins Sons & Co Ltd
London·Glasgow·Sydney·Auckland
Toronto·Johannesburg

First published 1989

A CIP catalogue record for this book
is available from the British Library.

ISBN 0 00 184683-3

Printed and bound in Belgium by
Proost International Book Production

What's that, Leo?

We've won a free night out at Rosso's Restaurant !
It says, "black tie"
But what else shall we wear?

Can I wear my cowboy trousers, Mum?
Anything for me?

We must hurry.
The taxi will be
here soon.

I'm excited!

Your coat, Madam.
Good evening, young man. I'm Mr Rosso.

You have good taste in cereals. Enjoy yourselves tonight.

This way
Sir.

May I recommend Rosso's raspberry rissoles ?
ROSSO'S
Menu

Look – a band! Are you going to have a dance, Mum?

Would Madam care for some dessert ?

Yes please – after a dance with you.
Moi ?

Mum! Put him down! I want my pudding!

You're a natural.
And so are you.

Look! Everyone's joining in. Come on, Leo!

Will you dance with me please ?
Madam, may I have the pleasure ?

This is more like it !

Aaaarrrgh.....! My diamond earring!

Don't worry.
I'll find it
for you.

Leo, come
and choose your
pudding!

That one, please.
What's this?

Well done, my boy. This calls for a round of Fizz Pop!

But what about my pudding ?

At last

May we offer you a lift home ?

Au revoir

Next morning...

ROSSO'S RESTAURANT

Last night went with such
a swing — please be my
guests again tonight.

Alphonso Rosso

Grandpa

PRINTED IN BELGIUM BY
proost
INTERNATIONAL BOOK PRODUCTION